TOO EARLY

Words by
NORA ERICSON

Pictures by
ELLY MACKAY

Abrams Books for Young Readers

New York

I wake up very early.

"Good morning, Mama. Good morning, Daddy."

"*Shhhh*, don't wake the baby."

Mama gives me sleepy kisses.

"Too early," Daddy groans,

feeling for his glasses, pulling on his robe.

"*Shhhh*, don't wake the baby."

Hurry hurry to the hall.

Shuffle shuffle down the stairs.

Daddy rubs his eyes. "You wake up too early."

Doggies yawn in their beds.
Snuffle snuffle, s-t-r-e-e-e-t-c-h-h-h
(Don't say it's too early, doggies—
I know you sleep all day!)

Burble burble goes the coffeepot. *Beep beep.*

(*Mmm*, it smells like morning. But just warm milk for me.)

Sip sip gulp goes Daddy. "You wake up too early."

Dark room, creaky floor.
"Let's sit on the porch."
He opens up the door.

Big sky, cool air.
Hello, Moon. You're lucky,
you get to stay up all night.

Daddy asks, "Can you find Venus?
She's the morning star, like you."
I know I can . . .

I do!
Good morning, Venus.
Do you wake up
too early, too?

Chilly feet. Steaming mugs. Quiet street.

Snuggle in, but watch your elbows.

(Careful not to bump the coffee!)

Black turns gray. I can almost see the mountains.

There they are!

Now the wind is waking.
Tickle tickle on my cheeks,
rustle rustle through the leaves.

Birds untuck and start to coo.
Whooo whooo, you wake up too early,
yes you doooo

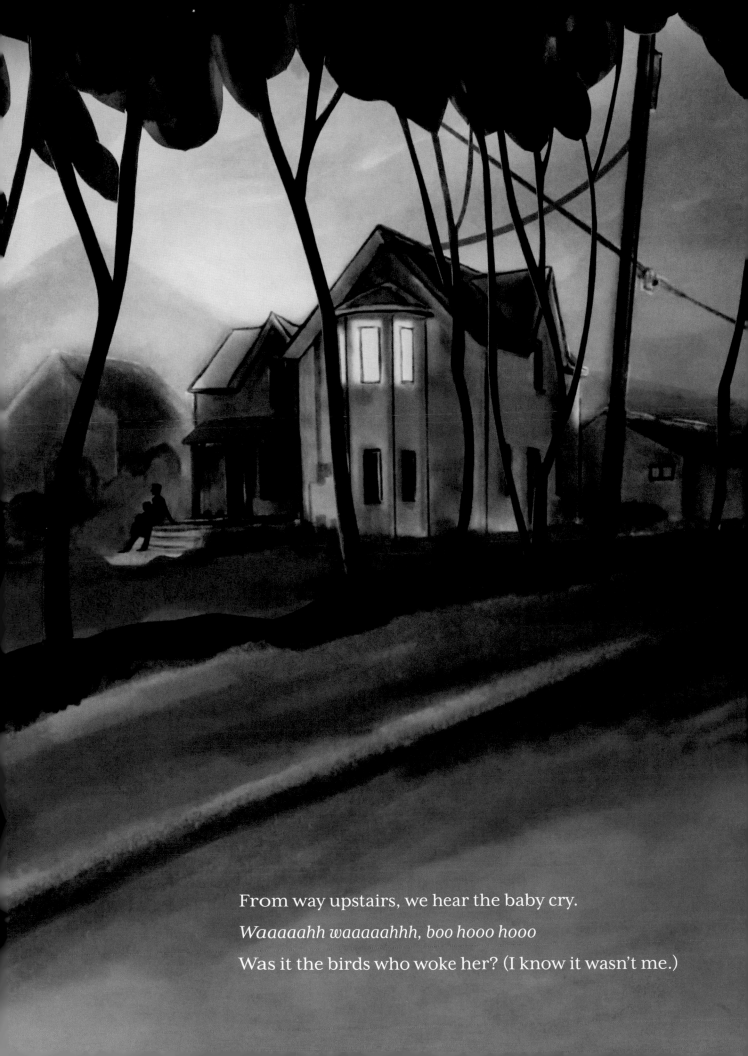

From way upstairs, we hear the baby cry.

Waaaaahh waaaaahhh, boo hooo hooo

Was it the birds who woke her? (I know it wasn't me.)

Gray turns purple. Stripes of pink.
Good morning, Sun, on your way at last.
You don't wake up nearly as early as I do.

Mama will be down soon, bringing baby, too.
Then all of us together,
    rush rush breakfast,
        rush rush clothes,
            rush rush school.

It won't feel so early anymore.

But right now, Daddy points.

"Look!"

A streak of white in the not-quite-light . . .

there . . . then gone . . .

a shooting star!

I shiver in my PJs, and Daddy pulls me closer in.

Fuzzy face, fuzzy hair, fuzzy robe.

"You sure do wake up early."

And yes, it's true. I wake up very early.

I wake up just in time.

For Max,
my partner at 4 a.m.
—N. E.

To my husband, Simon,
and our early risers
—E. M.

The illustrations for this book were drawn, cut, set up in layers, and photographed with light.

Cataloging-in-Publication Data has been applied for and may
be obtained from the Library of Congress.

ISBN 978-1-4197-4207-1

Text © 2022 Nora Ericson
Illustrations © 2022 Elly MacKay
Book design by Heather Kelly

Printed and bound in China
10 9 8 7 6 5 4 3 2 1

Abrams Books for Young Readers are available at special discounts when
purchased in quantity for premiums and promotions as well as fundraising
or educational use. Special editions can also be created to specification.
For details, contact specialsales@abramsbooks.com or the address below.

Abrams® is a registered trademark of Harry N. Abrams, Inc.

ABRAMS The Art of Books
195 Broadway, New York, NY 10007
abramsbooks.com